JAFTA
THE HOMECOMING

Story by Hugh Lewin - Pictures by Lisa Kopper

AN UMBRELLA BOOK   Alfred A. Knopf • New York

My father, said Jafta, is coming home.
He's been away for a very long time, but
Mother says things are changing in our
country and now he can come home.

I've missed him so much. He's been in the city, making
money for us, working down a deep hole in the ground,
and he's left a big hole in our lives.

But now maybe we can all live at home together and
begin to fill in what we've missed.

My father's missed so much that's happened
here. There was the big storm,

and the harvest, and he wasn't even here
for Nomsa's wedding.

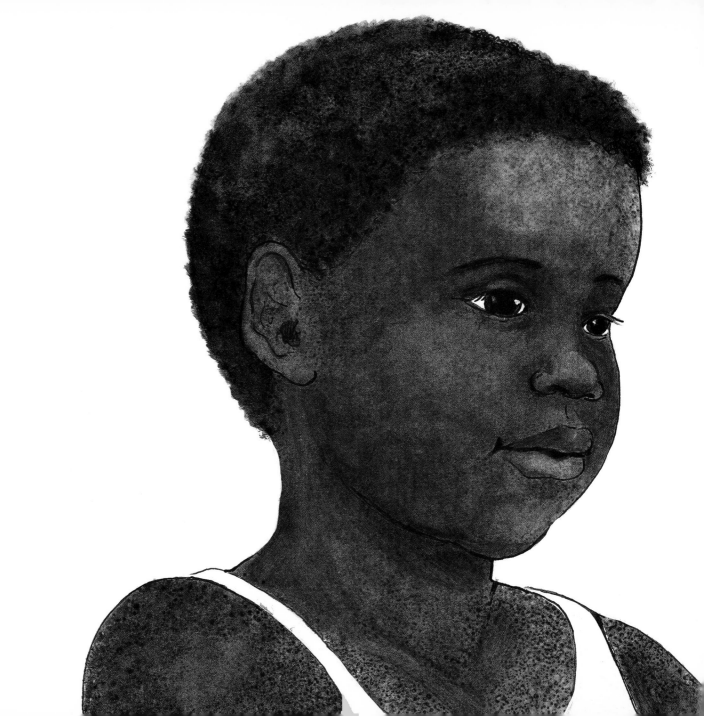

There's so much I wanted to show him.
Like the wounded hawk,

and Tombi when she was
small with sharp teeth,

and the bus I made for Thoko.

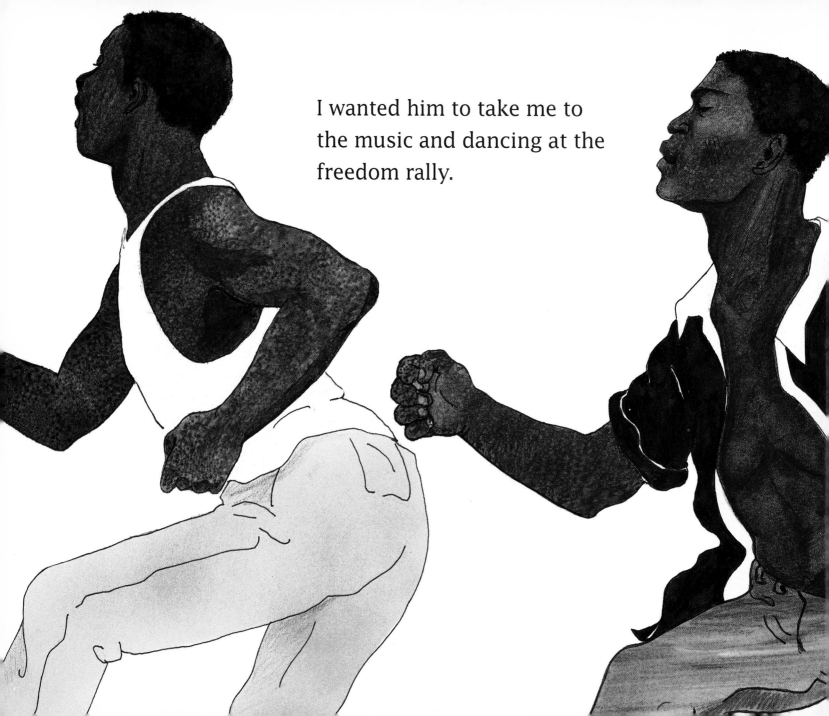

I wanted him to take me to the music and dancing at the freedom rally.

And I know he would have laughed when Sekuru
fell into the water. I love to hear him laugh.

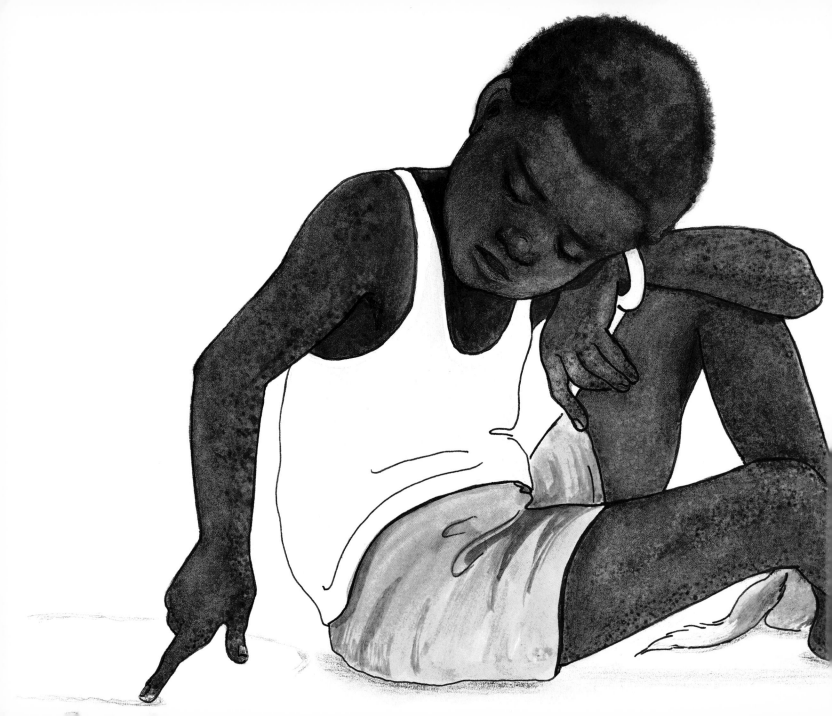

I wanted to tell him things, secret things that only he would understand. I wanted to ask him things that nobody else could answer. I wanted him to tell me why he had to work far away from home, away from us.

I wonder if he'll look any different. Will he think I've grown? Will he have presents for us and lots of stories to tell?

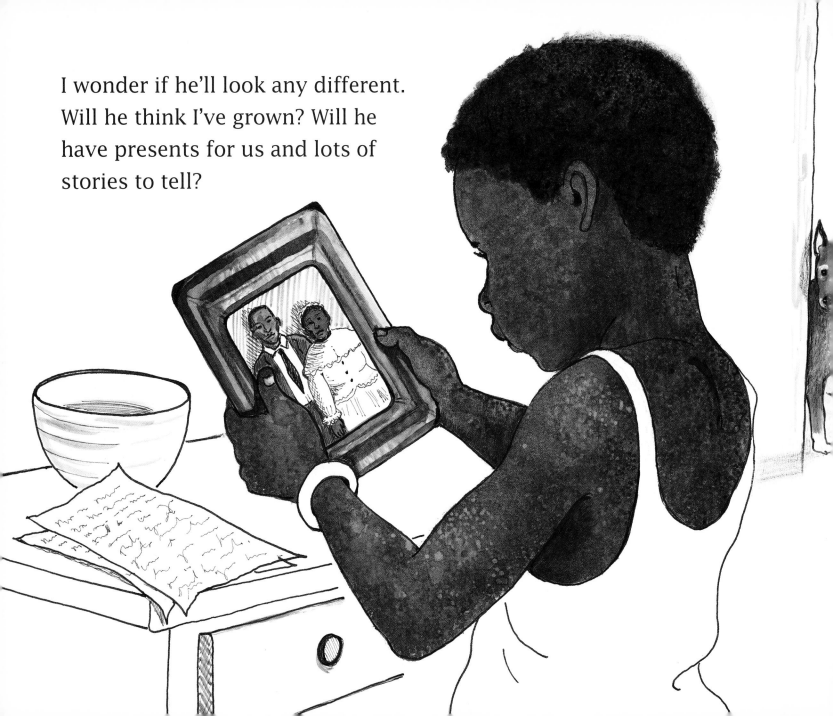

Mother says we'll have a homecoming party
bigger than at Nomsa's wedding.

Things are changing in our country and
my father's coming home...
coming home...
coming home...

My father's come home.

Library of Congress Cataloging-in-Publication Data

Lewin, Hugh.
Jafta—the homecoming / story by Hugh Lewin ; pictures by Lisa Kopper.
p.   cm. — (An Umbrella Book)
    Summary: A young black South African boy describes his feelings about
his father's return from working in the city.
ISBN 0-679-84722-7 (trade) — ISBN 0-679-94722-1 (lib. bdg.)
[1. Fathers and sons—Fiction. 2. South Africa—Fiction. 3. Blacks—South Africa—
Fiction.]   I. Kopper, Lisa, ill. II. Title. III. Series: Umbrella book
(New York, N.Y.)
PZ7.L58418Jak   1994   [E]—dc20 93-12945

Manufactured in the United States of America
10 9 8 7 6 5 4 3 2 1